This book belongs to …

....

Tips for Talking and Reading Together

Stories are an enjoyable and reassuring way of introducing children to new experiences.

Before you read the story:

- Talk about the title and the picture on the cover. Ask your child what they think the story might be about.
- Talk about a time when you have tried something new. Does your child go to any classes?

Read the story with your child. After you have read the story:

- Discuss the Talk About ideas on page 27.
- Talk about the different ballet positions on pages 28–29 and then try them out yourselves.
- Do the fun activity on page 30.

Have fun!

Find the 10 bugs hidden in the pictures.

For more hints and tips on helping your child become a successful and enthusiastic reader look at our website www.oxfordowl.co.uk.

Kipper's First Dance Class

Written by Roderick Hunt and Annemarie Young
Illustrated by Nick Schon, based on the original
characters created by Alex Brychta

OXFORD
UNIVERSITY PRESS

Sam and his dad came to see Kipper. Sam had something to ask. "I want to have ballet lessons," he said. "Will you come too?"

"Sam wants to be a footballer," said his dad.
"And ballet will help. It's really good for developing
strength and football moves."

Kipper wasn't sure he'd like going to dance classes.
"Please come. We'll have fun," said Sam.

In the end, Kipper agreed to have a go. He was
glad to see one of his other friends was there too.
Anna waved and came over.

The ballet class was fun. Mary, the teacher, made them do funny walks. Then they had to stop suddenly. It was hard not to fall over.

The children liked Mary's helper, Leo. When Mary asked everyone to make a scary shape with their arms, Leo made them all laugh.

A week later, Mary told the children to get into groups. "Think of an insect," she told them. "Then try to move just like that insect."

Kipper, Sam and Anna decided to be crickets. "We can crouch down and jump up suddenly," said Sam.

Jumping like a cricket was hard.

Leo showed the children
how to bend down
and then jump up.

"Now we'll add some music," said Mary. "Try to move in time to the music."

At the next lesson they learned how to skip.
"Hop on one leg, then step with the other," said Mary.
"That's right, Kipper. Well done."

Sam and Anna watched Kipper. Then they hopped and stepped. Soon they were all skipping.

"This is fun!" said Kipper.

The following week, Mary said, "You're very good at being insects, so we're going to do The Bugs Ballet for the end of term show."

Sam and Anna were excited. Kipper wasn't sure.

Then Leo said, "I'm going to dance too. I'm a wasp!"

"That'll be fun," said Kipper.

Mum and Anna's dad were making the cricket
costumes. The children were practising being crickets.
It was hard.

"We have to turn our legs out, not just our feet," said Kipper.

"We'll never do it!" said Sam.

"Yes we will," said Anna.

The end of term came and they were rehearsing for the show.

"Don't forget to smile as you dance," said Mary.

All the children skipped to the music, then the crickets jumped.

"We got it right!" said Kipper.

"Well done!" said Leo.

It was time for the show. All the parents came to watch.
Leo started the show. He did a dance with a girl
called Tasha.

Tasha was a butterfly who was caught in a spider's web.
Leo had to pull her free. They danced beautifully
and everyone clapped.

When it was their turn, Kipper, Anna and Sam started their Dance of the Crickets. They felt a bit nervous.

"Smile!" thought Kipper.

First they skipped, then they bent and jumped,
just like crickets!

"Bravo!" called Leo.

Everyone clapped and cheered.

"I didn't think insects could be so much fun," said Dad.
"Mind that wasp, Dad!" called Kipper.

Talk about the story

Why did Sam want to go to ballet lessons?

What did Anna, Sam and Kipper find hard to do?

Why did Kipper enjoy the ballet lessons in the end?

What insect would you choose to be in The Bugs Ballet?

Ballet positions

Anna is going to show you the five positions of the feet.
You can try these yourself.

First

Second

Third   Fourth   Fifth

Spot the difference

Find the five differences in the two costumes.

FIRST EXPERIENCES WITH Biff, Chip & Kipper

Have you read them all yet?

 Learning to Swim

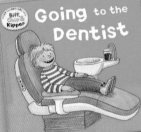 Going to the Dentist

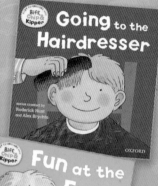 Going to the Hairdresser

Kipper's First Pet

 Going on a Plane

Let's Recycle!

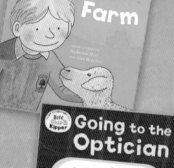 Fun at the Farm

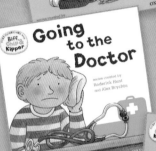 Going to the Doctor

 Kipper Gets Nits

 Going to the Hospital

 Going to the Optician

Starting School

FIRST EXPERIENCES Flashcards 55 cards

 Kipper's First Dance Class

 A New Baby

 Kipper's First Match

 Going to the Vet

Series created by Roderick Hunt and Alex Brychta

OXFORD

Read with Biff, Chip and Kipper
The UK's best-selling home reading series

	Phonics				First Stories			

Level 1
Getting ready to read
               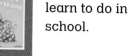

Level 2
Starting to read
             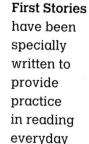

Level 3
Becoming a reader

Level 4
Developing as a reader

Level 5
Building confidence in reading

Level 6
Reading with confidence

Phonics stories help children practise their sounds and letters, as they learn to do in school.

First Stories have been specially written to provide practice in reading everyday language.

READ WITH Biff, Chip & Kipper

OXFORD
UNIVERSITY PRESS

Great Clarendon Street, Oxford OX2 6DP

Text © Roderick Hunt and Annemarie Young 2009
Illustrations © Nick Schon and Alex Brychta 2009
First published 2009
This edition published 2014

10 9 8 7 6 5 4 3 2 1
Series Editors: Kate Ruttle, Annemarie Young
British Library Cataloguing in Publication Data available
ISBN: 978-0-19-273677-2
Printed in China by Imago
The characters in this work are the original creation of Roderick Hunt and Alex Brychta who retain copyright in the characters
With thanks to Mary Schon ARAD and Henry Rhodes